MYSTERY SHORT STORY COLLECTION VOUME 1

CONNOR WHITELEY

No part of this book may be reproduced in any form or by any electronic or mechanical means. Including information storage, and retrieval systems, without written permission from the author except for the use of brief quotations in a book review.

This book is NOT legal, professional, medical, financial or any type of official advice.

Any questions about the book, rights licensing, or to contact the author, please email connorwhiteley@connorwhiteley.net

Copyright © 2022 CONNOR WHITELEY

All rights reserved.

DEDICATION

Thank you to all my readers without you I couldn't do what I love.

AUTHOR OF THE ENGLISH BETTIE
PRIVATE EYE SERIES

CONNOR WHITELEY

EMBEZZLER IN THE ROOM

AN AMATEUR SLEUTH MYSTERY SHORT STORY

EMBEZZLER IN THE ROOM

The criminal was here.

Penelope Froster hated the fact she had even had to arrange this little meeting on a wonderfully warm Friday evening that she would have loved to be spending with her husband, two adult children that were back from university, and their dog.

But oh no, because of some idiot who had been helping themselves to HER money, her business and her clients, Penelope had to sit here in her roomy boardroom with tall glass walls around them and sitting on uncomfortable chairs to find out who did it.

It had taken her ages to go through all the banking information, incidents and fake cheques that she had apparently made out to a number of companies. Penelope had no idea who would want to steal from her, she liked to think she was a wonderful person, helpful, respectful and someone who loved all of her employees.

Some people might have said owning a business

that made and distributed cat, dog and fish food to pet shops wasn't the sexiest business, but it paid well.

Penelope took off her long pink overcoat and pulled slightly at her white shirt, black trousers and even loosened her high-heels to make her comfortable. She didn't want to be the uncomfortable one here.

That was for the criminal.

The horrible smell of expensive aftershave hit Penelope in the face as her second in command Aron moved around in his own uncomfortable chair. Penelope loved his chisel handsome face and tight suit, it was one of the reasons why she had hired him, he was perfect to send into the female-led pet shops who had kicked Penelope out.

Penelope was pretty sure Aron could sell mice to elephants. He was that good.

As much as she didn't want to believe it was him, she couldn't deny the fact he had been job hunting, acting strange towards her and he did have access to her chequebook.

As the sounds of the air-conditioning humming, the outside traffic rushing past and the office's computer buzzing, Penelope hoped this wouldn't take too long. She really wanted to get back to her kids, but no one steals money from Penelope and gets to work at HER business.

When two women started tapping their long perfectly shaped nails on the table, Penelope glared at them. The one on the left was called Phoebe,

Penelope's secretary, and whilst she was great at her job, she always seemed a little weird to Penelope.

Not crazy weird, but the type of weird you start to understand when you realise that outside of work, they don't really have much of a life.

Normally Penelope loved people like that because it became part of her job and role as an employer to help these people. Penelope had taken Phoebe to music concerts, bars and other socials to try and get her to make friends.

It didn't work, but at least Penelope had tried.

Penelope wasn't sure it was Phoebe, she didn't want it to be her, but it wouldn't be hard for Phoebe to find copies of her signature to practice and copy from, and the dates and times of the fake cheques always seemed to match when Phoebe was out doing to an odd job for Penelope.

The woman on the right, Jasmine, was a much older woman about Penelope's age, late forties, with her greying hair in a mess and her dirty white shirt was loose.

It was far from the professionalism that Penelope wanted from her staff but she couldn't blame Jasmine too much. It was after hours on a wonderfully warm evening and like Penelope everyone here probably wanted to be gone and as far away from here as possible.

Penelope stood up and smiled. "Thank you everyone for staying. I really do appreciate it,"

Aron and Phoebe nodded with respect but

Jasmine stood up.

"What this about? I gotten go home,"

Penelope sat down and glared at Jasmine so she did the same. Penelope leant closer to them as if she was going to tell them all the start of some strange conspiracy.

And in a way she was. The conspiracy of how one of them was stealing from her.

"Someone is stealing from us. There is over twenty thousand pounds missing from our accounts. It started six months ago and is getting worse," Penelope said.

No reactions.

"It always happens the same way. Someone writes a fake cheque in my name to some company we have never dealt with. Then they pay it in online or sometimes in-person and then the money disappears,"

Everyone looked at each other.

"What this gonna do with us?"

"Jasmine, I want you three to help me. You're the only three I trust to help me," Penelope said.

Everyone smiled and technically it wasn't a lie, because Penelope had invited them here to help her and she fully believed by the end of this meeting, she would know who the criminal was. She just didn't want them knowing she suspected them. Yet.

"Have you gone to the police yet?" Aron asked.

"I have not. I wanted to give them something concrete first. I wanted them to act and not brush me aside,"

Phoebe pointed her finger at Penelope. "Completely understand. My brother was mugged straight after a terror attack and the police was too busy apparently,"

Penelope wasn't entirely sure how to respond to that, but it did prove her point at least. As much as she loved and supported the police, she did need to give them something. A confession would be nice but Penelope wasn't too hopeful.

"What days were the last few cheques done?" Aron asked.

Penelope took out her small notebook from her overcoat and opened it. "The last three cheques were made out on the 15th, 21st and 30th of last month. I called the bank and I suspect another cheque for today, the 5th,"

Everyone nodded.

Penelope wasn't sure what their nods meant, it was probably that they understood what she had said. But now she could hopefully catch them in a lie, someone had to be available on those dates to write, cash and benefit from the fake cheques.

"Who in the business was available?" Penelope asked.

"Me and the peeps were busy making the product every day. It can't be us," Jasmine said.

Penelope knew that was a lie because they didn't work every business day and at least two days a month they give tours for the production rooms for clients, and from what Penelope could remember Jasmine always took those days off.

"I always do your diaries and answer calls," Phoebe said.

Penelope checked her notebook again as she remembered something wasn't true about that.

"But you took the 15th and the 31st off," Penelope said smiling.

"Oh yeah, my dog was ill,"

"You don't have a dog," everyone said.

Phoebe looked at the door and Penelope just glared at her. "What did you do?"

"Nothing boss,"

Penelope's eyes narrowed.

"Fine," Phoebe said. "I was with Aron,"

Penelope cocked her head and looked at Aron. That made no sense, he was gay for starters which was why he was so perfect to send into the female-led shops to flirt with those businesses. There was no chance of him falling for the owners and telling them why he was there.

But that raised the question why was he with Phoebe?

Aron shook his head and frowned. "Boss I'm sorry,"

"Sorry for what?"

Aron and Phoebe exchanged glances, and Aron leant closer to Penelope. "You know you caught me looking for another job,"

"Yes,"

"I've been looking for a bank loan," Phoebe said.

Penelope couldn't believe this, both of her prized employees were looking to set up their own business, their own pet shop business and cut into her market, her profits, her life. She had been nothing but good to them. Penelope loved them as her second family.

And it made sense why they were embezzling from her business, they needed the money. But seriously! Stealing!

"Why are you setting up your own pet business?" Penelope asked.

The three suspected Embezzlers all looked at each other.

"What?" Penelope asked.

Aron cocked his head. "We aren't. We want to make you an offer,"

Penelope stood up and walked around the table a few times before she sat back down and stared at Aron.

"Boss, we love you and what you've done. Phoebe told me about your dreams to expand, offer more types of pet food and make even more. You wanted to go national, not regional," Aron said.

Penelope slowly nodded. That was all true, she had wanted to grow the business and develop it further. But it still didn't explain everything.

"Make me an offer?"

Jasmine started tapping her nails against the table.

"Boss both of us wanted to invest ten thousand

into the business. Become partners and help you," Aron said.

Now that made a bit more sense. Especially with twenty thousand pounds being two times ten, but why would they look for a bank loan, want to invest money, only to decide to embezzle it anyway.

"If ya both wanna invest it, why steal it?" Jasmine asked, clearly making the same connection as Penelope had.

Penelope nodded.

"We didn't boss. I scratched together my ten thousand, got some off my husband and… and Phoebe got some somehow," Aron said.

All eyes turned to Phoebe who was shaking. "I did not steal,"

Penelope stood up and stared at her. "Maybe you didn't see it as stealing, embezzling or anything. Maybe you saw it as borrowing some money you wanted to give back and invest. Am I getting closer?"

Phoebe's eyes turned watery. "I didn't do it. Honest. Pen I would never steal from you,"

Then out of the corner of Penelope's eyes she saw Jasmine smile. Penelope turned to her.

"Why are you smiling? Embezzler!" Penelope shouted.

The smile melted away from Jasmine's face being replaced with a deep horrible frown.

"So what you got to say for yourself?" Aron asked.

Jasmine leant back and put her feet on the table.

Penelope subtly slid her hand under the table to her coat's pocket and turned on the recorder on her phone.

"I donna know what ya talking about. It was Phoebe that give me the blank cheques,"

Phoebe shrugged.

"It was ya bossy that give ma the files I copied ya signature from," Jasmine said. "Ya all just stupid,"

"But why?" Penelope asked.

"Cos ya ungrateful. I wanna be partner. I wanna be great and powerful and independent. But na just cos I'm poorer than the rest of ya, I ain't able to become a partner,"

Penelope just shook her head at that reasoning. She didn't even want any partners in the business, at least she didn't think so, she loved her employees and everything they did for her. Penelope loved Jasmine for being an amazing producer of the pet food, she never wanted Jasmine to feel like this.

And yet she did. The real question was what was Penelope going to do now.

"Where's my money?" Penelope asked coldly.

Jasmine shrugged. "I donna know. Better get tha police involved. *Or not*,"

Penelope pointed a warning finger at Jasmine. "What do you mean *or not*?"

"I mean if ya get tha pigs involved. They're gonna know I laced the food with something special,"

"What!" Aron and Phoebe shouted as they shot up.

"Yea, I laced it with some coke. Ya getting some very active pets!"

Penelope shook her head and simply walked out of the board room and dialled the police. This wasn't going to end well but she couldn't allow anything to happen to any of her clients, the pets and hopefully her business.

But she doubted that she was going to survive this.

***

12 Months later

As Penelope, Aron and Phoebe left the courthouse and walked along the busy London path with all sorts of business people in suits, dresses and coats rushing past them, Penelope couldn't believe what had happened in the past year.

After calling the police Jasmine had been arrested, charged with a number of crimes and then there was the mass operation to stop any of the food getting to her clients.

Thankfully because of Phoebe's amazing organisation and Penelope's no-BS attitude, all of the contaminated food hadn't been sold to customers or given to any pets. So everywhere was safe and no one was harmed.

But for the rest of the year Penelope, Aron and Phoebe were in court most days defending themselves for lawsuits from clients to pet owners to all the vulture legal firms who wanted a "quick and easy win" for their clients.

It annoyed Penelope more than she wanted to admit how much money they had had to pay out in the past year. Penelope even had to sell the business and go job hunting just to keep the lights on.

It was amazing about even though no one was hurt, injured or poisoned, the world didn't seem to care too much. After the news reported her problem in the media, she knew she was done and her entire client list vanished overnight.

No one wants to work with a poisoner.

As she felt Aron and Phoebe rub her shoulders, Penelope looked at them and smelt the horrible London pollution in the air, but she loved seeing her friends' smiling faces.

But their smiles weren't the forced kind you get when people don't care but they still want to pretend to comfort you. They were truly caring smiles and it was almost like they wanted to give her something.

"Thanks you two for everything over the past year. I saved a few thousand for each of you as redundancy so I'll give you that and you two can get on with your lives," Penelope said.

To her surprise, Aron and Phoebe shook their heads rapidly and looked excited.

"We don't want it," Aron said.

"We wanted you to tell you. If you want you can reopen the business," Phoebe said.

Penelope's eyebrows raised. "How? I don't have the money, the clients or anything,"

Aron and Phoebe passed her a cheque for ten

thousand each.

"No. You can't," Penelope said trying to push their hands away.

"We wanted this a year ago. We still want it," Aron said.

Penelope took the cheques and looked at them, gently tapping them in her hands. "You really want to do this?"

Both of them just nodded and gently guided the cheques into Penelope's pocket and zipped them safely inside.

Then Penelope took both of their arms and they walked down the street discussing new and exciting ideas about their new business venture.

And for the first time in a whole year (maybe longer) Penelope actually felt great about life, sure she hated how Jasmine had almost stolen her entire business and then later destroyed it.

But as Penelope always said to her children sometimes you need to burn away the old dead trees to make room for something new to grow. And that was what Penelope fully intended to do, she wasn't going to waste this opportunity.

She was going to love Aron and Phoebe and she was going to build a better, stronger and larger business so they could all enjoy their lives and make the lives of their family, their clients and pet owners better.

Because in the end that was all that Penelope had ever wanted, and now she was going to make sure it happened.

    Because life's too short not to do what you love.

MYSTERY SHORT STORY COLLECTION VOUME 1

STEALING A CHANCE AT FREEDOM

I never wanted to steal anything, but when you're a mother of three children, two dogs and a useless husband that sees you as nothing more than a sex machine, stealing starts to get really, really tempting.

To normal people my life would seem perfectly happy, I have a wonderful family, a loving husband that buys me whatever I want and I get to live in the penthouse of a posh building in London.

To me my life is awful, yes I have a wonderful family and I love, love, love my kids. I will defend them to the end, my husband pays for my imprisonment and he buys me whatever I want so I obey him for a bit longer, and as for that wonderful penthouse.

It is my prison.

But my stupid husband allows me to leave every Tuesday afternoon for three hours of freedom. That is the only time I am allowed to live my life without any one of his security guards (my guards) watching me and protecting our kids. He is an absolute nob.

As I stood against a cold marble wall next to the posh glass doors of a top London bank, I forced my hands not to shake because I knew if my husband found out why I was here, I would have an accident for sure, and he would desperately try to save me, but be sadly too late.

Oh yes, I have thought about this many a times because I know what my husband's like, that and he's had two other wives that mysteriously died on their honeymoon.

At least I beat them by ten years, but I know my time is running out.

The sound of posh bankers and other nobs muttering, talking and chatting with their thick accents were right in my ears as they proudly marched out of the bank, and then more and more people walked in.

This was the quietest the bank was ever going to yet so I had to start my mission soon.

The smell of posh nobs earthy aftershave, fine perfume and other disgusting things only reminded me of why I hated my husband, for all these men and a few women were the same. They poured on the smelly stuff to hide their corruption and awful business underneath.

But I had to steal my chance at freedom, I had to get my kids away from my husband even if it killed me.

I straighten my posh black dress, checked my

blond hair and balanced myself on my high heels before I walked into the crowd of bankers and went to the counter.

Even I had to admit the black marble of the large counter was impressive, very expensive and just wonderful in all honesty, and as I predicted there was a young cute man standing there. I had no idea how he had gotten a job at such a posh bank, it was clearly through a family connection (yet more corruption), yet I hoped he could help me.

You see all I needed was to get into the bank vault (fat chance of that you must be thinking) but this is where I have been spending my Tuesday afternoons for months, so I like to think I'm prepared.

"Hello Mrs, how may I help you?" the young man said with a massive smile.

Poor sod, the banking world would easily chew him up in the end.

"Hello kind sir, I would like to access mine and my husband's safety deposit box," I said sounding as posh and snobby as I could. It was rather easy.

"Of course Mrs, your name?"

"Mrs Annie Franklie,"

He looked down and I presumed he was checking something on his computer.

"I'm sorry Mrs but your husband has removed you from the account. Good day," he said.

The bastard!

Well that does settle it nicely, if there was a

shadow of a doubt in my mind about stealing all the idiot's money, I'm definitely going to do it now.

This was outrageous, I am his wife! I deserve every penny of his for my imprisonment. And if I was as stupid as him I would go to the police, but that idiot of an husband is so powerful, popular and posh his slimy words would be worth gold compared to mine.

I was going to steal everything!

Thankfully I was more than prepared for such an event. "I'm sorry about that kind sir. May I access my own safety deposit box?"

Then the young stuck-up man had the outrageous idea of looking down at me.

"*You* have a box?" he said.

"Of course kind sir, I opened it with your senior manager. I can phone him and get him to come down here immediately," I lied.

The young man smiled, checked his computer and called over another member of staff.

The young woman he called looked half surprised, brand new and completely shocked that she was having to do some work. But I couldn't help but feel like there was something going on with her, she didn't look, feel or smell like a typical banker or staff.

"Mrs Annie Franklie," I said to the young woman.

"Yes Gill please take the lady to the vault," the young man said.

Gill bowed and led me through the bank. I tried

my best not to bump into any of them as we both headed towards the back of the lobby through a gold door and into some black lifts. But that was just difficult.

When we went into the lift along with plenty of other smelly large bankers, my heart raced when I saw my husband step into the lift.

He moved through the crowd and stood right next to me, I stared at his evil stunningly dark eyes, tight black suit that left little to the imagination and that movie star smile that would melt any woman's heart.

The lift started to go down.

My husband's mouth went closer to my ear. "I was wondering when you would go to your box. I liked the money, passports and coffee in it,"

My world just stopped, my normal Tuesday afternoon (as stupid as it sounded) was I would go down privately into the bank vault open my box and make myself a wonderful cup of coffee.

It was only the cup of coffee I had in the week that wasn't poisoned, drugged or surrounded by my husband's corrupting touch. The bank vault gave me an amazing chance to just breathe for those three hours before I went back and got a beating for being five minutes late.

But none of this was over until I said so.

The lift stopped and all the other bankers got out so it was just me, Gill and my dick of a husband as the lift started to descend once more.

"Don't worry babe I shredded the passports, cashed the money and drank that coffee. You're nice and safe now my precious little girl,"

I should also note here that I am actually a year older than him, but for some reason the idiot likes to believe I am beneath him.

"Here we are," Gill said perfectly happy, as the lift door opens revealing a large room filled with hundreds if not thousands of tiny doors, where the safety deposits boxes were safely stored.

The only actual thing in the room was a large silver table that I had spent many an afternoon sitting on contemplating my life.

My husband grabbed my arm and he forced me into the room, I gagged at the smell of oil, chemicals and lemons that left a horrific taste in my mouth. I kept wanting Gill to say something or do something, but she was completely unaware of what was happening.

Gill took out the bank key. "Where is your box Mrs Franklie?"

I stayed silent. My husband squeezed tighter. I didn't speak.

"You okay Mrs Franklie?" she said smiling.

I still didn't say anything. My husband grabbed me with his other arm. Squeezing tighter.

My eyes watered.

"Mrs Franklie, I am here to help you," she said firmly.

My husband squeezed my arms as tight as he

could. Tears rolled down my face.

"Mrs Franklie, I am here to help you," she said extremely firm.

"Then help me!" I shouted.

Gill smiled.

Flying across the room.

She jumped into the air.

My husband released me.

I dashed forward.

Gill kicked him.

My husband fell back.

Gill landed.

She charged over to him.

Grabbing him by the throat.

Squeezing.

He kicked her.

He whacked her.

He smashed her into the wall

I jumped on him.

He slammed me into the wall.

I screamed.

He turned.

Kicking me in the stomach.

Crippling pain filled me.

A knife slashed his throat.

As my husband grabbed his throat and tried to stop the bleeding and then fell to the ground, I stared wide-eyed at Gill who was wiping the blood covered knife on the inside of her clothes.

She offered me a hand.

"Thank you?"

Gill double checked my husband was dead and took his bank key. "Your welcome, which one is his?"

"Number 1-4-5," I said.

She unlocked it, placed it on the table and opened it. I gasped as I saw thousands of pounds wrapped up together, photos and various legal documents inside.

Gill picked up a few bundles of money and offered it to me. I took it.

"What was your plan?" Gill asked as she stuffed the money into a black handbag she got from her pocket.

I smiled. "I planned to open my box, knock you out and steal some of the stuff from the other boxes,"

"I would like to see you try," she said smiling. "How did you get the equipment in needed to steal from the other boxes,"

"The bank doesn't check what my husband brings in. I simply give him a bag or two of cash each week. The bag contains cash and some items,"

Gill laughed as she pulled out various cutters, lock picks and other criminal things as she emptied my husband's box.

"But who are you?" I asked.

Gill shrugged. "A thief, assassin, a crook. Whatever I needed to be in the moment,"

"And your plan for today?"

"Well I didn't want to be serving you," she said coldly. "But I glad I did,"

I could only nod to that. She really had done me a favour, at least now I didn't need to worry about running away to a place where my husband couldn't touch me.

Gill took a few steps closer to me and pointed the knife at me. My eyes widened.

"Want to make sure you never get suspected?" she asked.

I was about to nod but I needed to know something first. "Why are you helping me?"

She took a deep breath. "Because I could have saved my sister once but I didn't. She was killed by a man like your husband. I can't let that happen again. Ready?"

I nodded.

She rammed the blade into my stomach and ran off.

As I collapsed to the floor and felt the blood gush out of me, I actually smiled as I knew that I was free, I was going to be a good mother once again and now I could actually go out into the world on other days that weren't Tuesday afternoon.

***

A week later after I was discharged from the hospital, the police kindly drove me back to my penthouse apartment when the kids were at school and I stood in front of my massive glass windows.

From his penthouse I could see all of London, I could see all the landmarks, all the ships on the river and everything I could ever want was now mine.

My penthouse (my prison no more) smelt wonderful of some of my favourite cinnamon candles (that he hated) and all I could hear was all the silence that came with my freedom. I no longer had to listen to the controlling silence where if I made a noise I was shouted or beaten, and I didn't feel like he was there to control me anymore.

Of course, all the legal paperwork was already in the post, I had done that in my hospital bed and spoke to the lawyers so everything was now mine, and no one, absolutely no one could ever take it away from me.

Of course I still wondered why I wanted to keep the penthouse that was my prison for so long, but this was my home and most importantly it was my kids' home and I was going to keep it for their sake.

Because that was why I did all of this, I did it for them, I did it for my freedom, my kids' freedom and most importantly so we could all live a better life.

So I might not have stolen a chance at freedom.

But I definitely killed a chance at my freedom.

And here I am, ready to enjoy it.

MYSTERY SHORT STORY COLLECTION VOUME 1

MATED AT THE MORGUE

This was bad! This was so so bad!

In all my life I have never been in such a bad situation, because I am currently paralysed and laying on a fucking morgue table.

Now I do not blame you in the slightest for not exactly knowing what it feels like, but for starters, I'm not dead. I'm just very, very paralysed which is horrific in itself. And to make matters even worse, the massive metal slab of a morgue table I'm currently on is freezing cold.

I mean it must have been put in a freezer overnight, because I am freezing here, and I'm deadly certain (probably not the best idea to use *deadly* in a place like this) that if I could move I would be shivering.

But sadly I am completely paralysed and the strangest thing about all of this is whenever the morgue attendees come in they talk about me like I'm dead and I'm about to be sliced into.

Personally I really don't like the idea of that, I don't know about you, but I don't like being thought of as dead when I'm very much alive. And to make matters worse, the entire morgue smells so horrible of extremely strong orange, cloves and clementine scented chemicals.

I don't want to have to breathe in all that until one of two things happens. Even a very smart person realises I'm alive and they help me. Or the admittedly (and far more) terrifying option is someone cuts me open and then I die.

Truly.

So as I laid here and stare up at the massive white ceiling with a massive white light shining overhead, which I took as a massive cruel joke, I was seriously starting to doubt I would ever survive.

In all honesty I'm not even too sure how I ended up in such a situation. I'm an office worker you see by day and I work in a massive investment bank doing computers, accounts and admin things. It is actually a lot more interesting than it sounds, and because I helped the CEO get a few million pounds of investment yesterday. I went out for drinks with my friends.

We went out for dinner first, of course, because I learn during university that dinner was critical if you want to spend all night drinking. And that's a very pro tip.

But I suppose things started to become a problem when I was on my tenth cocktail (and the real key there is not to mix drinks!) and my mouth started to burn and I could taste my golden chicken goujons and crispy juicy deep fried chicken.

Then I woke up here.

The only thing I can possibly think of was I can vomited, become paralysed and now I was here in this morgue on a wonderfully cold slab on a Saturday morning instead of in my bed, hopefully with a gay guy that I picked up the night before.

The sound of some kind of door opening made me want to look around, blink and do something else. But that was impossible and I really wanted to scream when an elderly man with a face covered in ache looked at me and licked his lips.

I wanted to really fucking scream then!

"Don't worry," the elderly man said, "the good Doctor will find out what happened to you,"

I wanted to shout at him and tell him I didn't need anything because I was alive, fit and very well. I didn't need him doing anything to me.

"Doctor," the elderly man said dipping his head slightly.

If I could move I would have breathed a sigh of relief when I saw this man was only a volunteer helper. But I wasn't exactly sure if that was very comforting, because who the hell volunteers to help out at a morgue in their retirement!

"Thank you Wilfred," presumably the doctor said.

I just wanted to roll my eyes. *Wilfred.* I'm sorry

but that was such a stupid name and so old fashioned, and when I saw *Wilfred* walk away I was seriously happy.

"That will be all today, Wil. I'll deal with this body and if anyone more come in over the weekend I'll deal with them on Monday. Go home and enjoy the weekend," presumably the doctor said.

"You sure doc?"

I didn't know what the doctor did, but I really hoped he only nodded as I heard the door shut behind Wilfred.

Then it locked.

Now I am no expert in doors, how they work and how they lock. But I am extremely sure morgues and their doctors and their dead patients wouldn't have a reason to be locked in the same room together.

I seriously didn't want to be here anymore!

A few moments later the massive white light moved away from my face and focused on my chest, and... wow?

I was staring at a seriously hot sexy man with an angular face, model-like looks and the most stunning emerald green eyes I had ever seen. This man was hot!

Yet I was a little unsure of him because he looked so young (about my age to be honest), so I couldn't understand how he was a doctor and was conducting autopsies all by himself.

But god this man was hot.

The Doctor smiled at me as he looked into my

unmoving, paralysed eyes. Then he checked my patient information, presumably from the police and paramedics.

"Mr Luke Ashley," the doctor said, "you're quite the looker, and I locked the door so we can have some privacy,"

Shit!

This was just my fucking luck wasn't it. I wasn't actually dead, I was alive and I was going to be "touched up" by a doctor that liked dead bodies. What the fuck!

I really, really tried to lift a finger, blink and kick. But nothing was moving, I was perfectly alive and there was no way to prove it.

The Doctor gently ran a finger down my slightly muscular chest and my slightly six-pack abs, and then I felt his finger hit something. Then I realise was I extremely grateful for the towel covering my lower section.

"You know Luke," the Doctor said, "you actually remind me a little of my ex-boyfriend. He left me a few weeks ago when I graduated medical school,"

Now I felt so stupid for really wanting to shiver with excitement at the way he said my name. He sounded so sexy, charming- and utterly creepy as I saw him trying to decide which scalpel to use to cut me open.

I had to do something!

"And I'm sorry. I'm Doctor Calum Limestone and I'm covering the current doctor whilst he's on holiday for the weekend," he said.

I had to admit Calum was a good name, and he did look great.

Calum pressed the cold scalpel against my chest and I really wanted to scream, lash out or just do something to stop him.

"If you were alive, I would never do this to you. You're beautiful and I'm sure you have an interesting life. It's wrong that great looking guys like you die,"

I'm not fucking dead genius!

The scalpel sliced into my flesh and I felt my bright red blood drip down my sides onto the freezing cold morgue slab I was resting on.

"Wait," Calum said gently. Then he started to inspect the blood.

He might be starting to understand.

Calum sliced a bit more.

Fucking idiot!

More blood dripped out of the wound. I just wanted to scream.

"This isn't right. That's a lot of blood and it's too bright for this to be normal," Calum said.

No shit Sherlock!

Calum just shook his head like he was overreacting and sliced a bit more. I felt more blood drip down my sides and even pool slightly on my chest.

"Shit!" Calum said.

Then he instantly started to apply pressure to *his* slices and his stunning emerald eyes just stared into mine.

Calum weakly smiled. "I'm sorry. I'll fix this. I won't let you die,"

***

I didn't know how long I had been out (well, not in the gay sense at least), but when I opened my eyes slowly. Bright natural sunlight shone through a massive floor-to-ceiling window and I was thankfully in a very comfortable hospital bed with fine sheets, a comfortable pillow and various pieces of equipment all around me.

The entire place smelt great with hints of lavender, roses and tulips filling the air and I was really glad to be out in the land of the living.

And I could move!

I raised my hand in front of my face and just focused on how great it felt to be able to move my fingers, toes and arms. It was such a great feeling.

The sound of the equipment humming, buzzing and beeping was actually a good reminder of what normal life sounded like instead of the cold silence of the morgue.

Then I looked at the massive window and saw a very hot man looking back at me. I wasn't sure why Doctor Calum was here, but I was rather glad he was, even after he kept cutting into me.

There was just something about his amazing smile, emerald eyes and his angular face that I just loved. And I seriously just wanted to ask him out and see where the future might take us.

Calum slowly walked towards me and sat down on a wooden chair that I hadn't noticed before was sitting there by my bed.

"I am sorry," he said.

"Sorry about the privacy and locking the door," I said, smiling.

Calum looked so scared for a few moments, but then he smiled too.

"You were awake then? How long?" he asked.

"All of it. But that elderly man's creepy," I said.

Calum laughed. "Yea. That's why they rejected him at the hospital. But I'm really glad you're okay,"

"What happened to me? How long was I out for?" I asked.

Calum gestured if he could take my hand and I didn't even hesitate.

"This might be hard for you to hear," Calum said, slowly rubbing my hand. I loved the feeling of his hands against mine. "You were poisoned on your night out by your CEO,"

It was amazing to feel my eyebrows rise as he said that.

"Turns out your CEO felt embarrassed by your success, and he was a bit psychotic anyway. So he poisoned you and planned to watch your paralysed face as he killed you later on,"

I held his hand tighter.

"Thankfully the poison acted too quickly and your friends got the cops involved. So you were declared dead, the police investigated and your boss was arrested,"

I just nodded. At least I would never have to worry about him again.

"Thanks for waiting for me," I said, I managed to surprise myself at that.

When I first met this amazingly hot man, I had been terrified of being "touched up" and more as he believed I was dead. Then I believed I was going to be killed by him. And now… and now I really wanted to him.

This definitely has to be the weirdest meet-cue in history.

Calum lent closer. "I know you… you might not be into men. But I was wondering-"

I couldn't help but laugh as Calum turned all nervous, shaky and like he was a little schoolboy again.

"Yes," I said. "I'll go on a second date with you,"

"Second?" he asked.

I just smiled. "You saw me naked in the morgue. That's a date to me,"

Calum laughed and he really had the cutest laugh ever, and I loved it.

As we kept talking, laughing and smiling at each other like two teenage boys, I never thought I would meet my soulmate like this. But I was so glad I had, Calum was an amazing guy and I was really, really looking forward to the future.

And spending the rest of my life with this man who always made me feel utterly amazing.

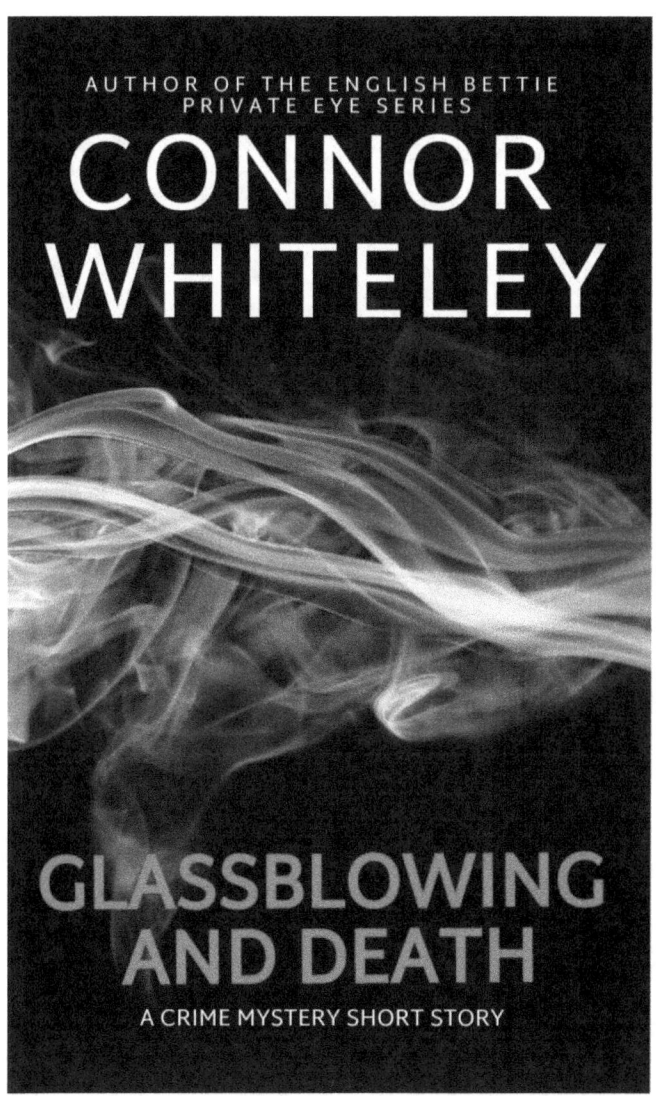

GLASSBLOWING AND DEATH

This was the day I became a killer.

I really forget when I became a glassblower or got interested in the whole area, maybe around the age of 12 so easily a decade ago, and I really, really love it.

It is truly amazing how I can melt down stunning glass into a molten mess and then transform that mess into something breathtaking. Of course others could probably (and do) do it better, but I still love creating stunning objects from glass.

I love creating objects for clients even more because it's wonderful to see their wide eyes light up as I give them my creations, I almost love their eyes lighting up as much as I love the clapping, cheers and ahs that they always give me.

Now I wouldn't blame you in the slightest if you thought I was some Grand Master or celebrity in the glass blowing world, but that honour is far, far, far from mine.

As I walked into my massive black-walled workshop with an immense furnace one side and three long workbenches lining the other sides, I instantly smiled. Being here always made me smile and be filled with so much happiness because this place was magical.

Just like a woodcarver being able to turn logs into breath-taking decorations, I like to think I can transform a molten mess into pure stunning objects, like the glasses I'll be making today.

Before I started the furnace for the day's work, an amazing array of glasses caught my eye on one of the tables. I couldn't believe how stunning the glasses were with their strips of baby blue, blood red and bright green running through it to create an amazing pattern.

I wish I could do something so creative and wonderful, then it dawned on me who had created them.

You see in the glass blowing world (of all places) there is a small but powerful hierarchy, you have the apprentices that were treated as cleaners (I'm so glad I'm no longer one of them), then you have the workers like me, and finally you have the celebrities.

All these people are are the people who are won rewards, are celebrated for their mastery and I hate them!

I spend every day in this smelly hot place, I submit for all the major rewards and I learn everything I can about glassblowing, but oh no, I still can't even get the judges to give my stuff a real look. All they do is quickly dust over it and go on to look at the celebrity's stuff.

Rubbish!

My stuff is amazing and I'm going to prove it to them this year!

And by them, I mean the National Glass Blowing Championship that is thankfully being held here in Bath, England, so at least there's no risk of my stuff getting smashed along the way up to London.

But if that wasn't bad enough, this was the final year of the stupid championships, so if I failed this year then I would fail for life. I want to win, I need to win, I want my skills to be recognised.

I shook my head and realised that I just needed to focus, so I went over to the immense black furnace, I dusted off the control panel that was filled with buttons, switches and electronic readings. Then I pressed one of the cold buttons a few times and the furnace lit.

A massive whoosh echoed around the workshop as the furnace and the crackling of flames filled the workshop as the day was truly beginning.

I was about to start selecting my glass bars for the day when the workshop door opened and a tall skinny man came in wearing his normal apron, protective gear and this stupid smile. The man the celebrity of the workshop, the man who won all the awards and could do anything he wanted because he kept the clients coming in, for he was Mr Dean

Lawson.

In all honesty, he wasn't such a bad man, we used to get along alright until he didn't think of me as worthy enough to invite to his annual award unveiling, in other words, a chance for him to show off all his awards.

It also probably didn't help that I had called in a cheater in public and destroyed my reputation in a single second. That was a massive mistake, but I was a good glassblower!

"Alright Sean," he said to me as he picked out his glass bars for his first piece.

All I could do was nod and then I checked the clock and frowned, it was nine o'clock that meant the workday had started and I would have to wait until afterwards to start, try and probably fail in creating my masterpiece.

Of course Dean could create his masterpieces through the working day if he wanted to, but for me and the rest of the workers we had to create tourist things and fulfil the rest of the orders if we wanted to keep our jobs.

As I started to get out my equipment, melt my glass and shape it, my eyes kept flickering back to Dean and what he was doing. All of his amazing movements looked so artful, easy and elegant. Whereas I just looked like an utter idiot and such an amateur glassblower.

The warm flames engulfed the molten glass and I loved the feeling of the immense heat coming out of the furnace, it might have been the dead of winter outside but in here it was wonderfully warm.

The only slightly concerning thing about being so close to a furnace was I knew how easily it could destroy a human body completely, so there would be nothing for any cops, medical examiners or health and safety investigators to find.

I continued shaping the glass when I heard someone else walk into the workshop and started asking Dean some questions. I could tell by the voice it was the new apprentice we had, I think his name was Nate. I didn't know.

I kept blowing the glass as my eyes flicked over to them and Dean was (surprisingly) being extremely kind and good to Nate, he was being so nurturing, explaining how things worked and how to improve as a blower.

Pop!

I swore under my breath as my glass blew up and I had to start all over again. At this rate I was going to have to work overtime just to finish my work for the day, I had to focus.

"Sean, I'm working on an expensive piece for a top client. Mine if Nate works with you?" Dean said.

I hated how he could make everything sound so kind, elegant and intelligent, and of course *he* would be working on a top piece. I had to win this award.

I blew into the glass a bit more before looking at Dean.

"Sure," I said.

I supposed I couldn't have been too rude about it, when I was in Nate's position all I wanted was to be respected and learn, so I guess I had to try to give him that.

Pop!

This was really starting to annoy me! The air must have gotten too hot, expanded and cracked.

I just decided that I needed to start over so I smashed the glass into my waste bucket and got Nate to bring over some more glass.

When he passed me the glass, I had to admit in the flicking light of the flames he was really good looking, he was probably about a year or two younger than me. He was extremely fit, and with his brown hair parted to the left, amazing jawline and dark walnut eyes, he looked good.

"I'm making some fine glasses for the boss today. Have you made them before?" I asked.

Nate smiled. "Yes, could I do one by myself?"

As soon as he said that I was hesitant, if he just started doing it by himself then he might start making mistake after mistake and that would cost me time. I didn't have time to keep wasting on mistakes and breakages, I needed to finish early so I could start on my award winning piece.

But I was an apprentice once and I knew how hard they wanted to prove themselves.

"Sure," I said as I passed Nate the equipment and he started melting the glass.

As he melted, shaped and blowed it, I had to

admit he was rather good at this actually. His movements were purposeful, controlled and rather precise. I was not going to enjoy today if even Nate was better than me.

"Here's the shape," Nate said.

Wow! To normal people, it would have only looked like Nate had a massive colourful bubble with two long stems at each end, but to me it was great. All we had to do now was carefully cut the bubble and then where I'd cut would be where you pressed the glass against your lips. (of course after I dulled the edges!)

I nodded. "Great. Now slowly bring it out of the furnace, hold it over the waste bucket and I'll cut it."

He did it slowly and carefully and as I cut the glass, Dean smashed something, Nate jumped and my cutters went wrong.

Nate's glass smashed into the waste buckets below.

Personally I just wanted to shout at both Nate and Dean, they were clearly working together to stop me from creating a masterpiece. I didn't need their time wasting, I had to get back to work, finish the glasses and start working on my masterpiece.

But when I looked at Dean he wasn't looking happy as he stared into his own waste bucket, it clearly wasn't purposeful. Nate still should have known better to jump like that.

"Sorry," Nate said. "Do you want to take over?"

As much as I wanted him and Dean gone, I had

to help Nate learn the tricks of glass blowing so I shook my head and allowed him to continue.

Over the course of the next few hours, I was really impressed with Nate's skills, he was masterful, careful and had a great skill for blowing in a way that would shape the glass exactly how he wanted it.

I wish I had that skill.

But as he finished up the final glass, my mind started to turn to my masterpiece. I think it had to be something skilful, hard to do and something that would wow the judges. Maybe a dragon or phoenix with unique colours.

I quickly glanced over to our range of glass bars and was hardly impressed, there was nothing special there. There were no unique or dazzling colours, just the normal range that every other stupid contestant would be using.

I needed something amazing.

"Done," Nate said as he moved all the glasses he had done over to one of the tables so they could cool overnight.

As I smiled at him I looked around and frowned when I saw that Dean wasn't there, that was strange. But when I looked at the time, I realised it really wasn't that strange at all.

It was an hour past the end of my shift.

I had been so engrossed in helping Nate learn the skills, become a better glassblower and being such a good person that it had cut into *my* time. This was my time to create a masterpiece that would transform my career and help me get every single award I ever could have dreamed of.

Nate got out his phone and swipe it a few times, but I was far too annoyed to do anything else tonight so I went over to the control panel and switched off the furnace.

A massive whoosh echoed around the workshop.

Nate dropped his phone in the waste bucket.

He reached down.

I tried to warn him.

It was too late. I heard him hiss as a massive glass shard sliced into his hand and blood gushed out.

But when I went over to the waste bucket, I could only smile as I watched the blood mix with cold and partly-molten chunks of glass. It produced such a strange, unique colour that I just loved, it was amazing.

It was what I needed to create my masterpiece.

"Hey Nate, does anyone know you're here after work?" I asked kindly. "Do you need a lift back?"

"No thanks. Parents always know I leave straight after shift. They probably think I'm walking along the canals to get home,"

That was very good news for me, there were no cameras or security along the miles upon miles of canals. It would be perfectly possible for Nate to walk all that way and no one would see him, especially in the dead of winter.

I carefully picked up a massive cold shard of glass and smiled at him.

"Thank you,"
I slit his throat and fired up the furnace.

***

A month later I couldn't help my smile as I looked at the massive glass dragon and my award next to it. I couldn't be happier with the judges' comments about the breath-taking colour, the skill and the utterly amazing craftsmanship that I had shown.

Apparently I was a credit to the field with my unique use of colour.

Of course I felt a little bad about killing poor Nate but it was worth it. After I killed him, I poured as much of his blood as I could into the waste bucket, melted the glass and created my dragon. It didn't take anywhere near as long as I feared and now I was award winning.

No one would ever find the body, I threw Nate into the furnace after I was done and watched his body be reduced to ashes, and it was beautiful.

That was how I wanted to go out when the time came.

But right now I had to go to a major workshop to teach some hot new things about the art of glass blowing, go to lunch with all the other glass blowing celebrities and even spent my half-a-million pounds prize money.

Who knew murder could be so great?

MYSTERY SHORT STORY COLLECTION VOUME 1

THEFT OF INDEPENDENCE

Detective Amy Sawkins loved everything about the wonderful night, there was such a sense of magic, freedom and utter celebration in the air as all of Scotland celebrated their freedom.

Amy loved that Scotland, after centuries of slavery to England, was now free. It was amazing that decades of fighting peacefully, demanding freedom and standing up for the rights of Scottish people had finally given them their freedom.

Amy might not have been born in Scotland (she was born in awful England to her horror) but after living here for two decades and hating UK politics and how they abused Scotland so badly, she was extremely glad to be living in a free country.

Even now she had no idea why she moved to Scotland in the first place, she was perfectly okay in London, but she never wanted to be okay, she wanted to thrive, be happy and be loved. And that was why Scotland was her home, and she wouldn't have it any other way.

The smell of gunpowder shattered Amy's celebration focus as she snapped back into the crime scene where she was, she didn't want to be investigating a crime on this night. She wanted to be in the streets with her family, friends and boyfriend celebrating Scotland's achievement.

But oh no, because some idiot had decided to break into a government building, Amy was stuck with some crime scene techs whilst the rest of the country partied like their lives depended on it. Amy was not impressed.

As she looked around the smooth marble walls of the little box room she was in, Amy hated the cold of the wind blowing in through the shattered window, and the crime scene techs took photos, dusted for prints and gathered whatever evidence they could.

Hints of horrible gunpowder, bitter coffee and even some fruit cake assaulted Amy's senses as she stared at the remains of a wooden desk that once stood there, she wasn't sure the purpose of the building, let alone what was housed in the office.

But Amy's eyes narrowed on a wall safe that was wide open and had clearly been emptied out. The massive black marks on the safe's door told Amy everything she needed to know, and it just sickened her.

Someone had taken advantage of the nation's freedom, partying and celebrating to attack this place and steal from the Scottish Government. If the crime had taken place any other time, Amy wouldn't have been impressed.

Yet it happened today of all days so she was fuming. It was disgusting anyone would dare attack the Scottish Government today, to Amy this wasn't just an attack on her Government, this was an attack on her people (or at least her adoptive people).

When Amy heard the crime scene techs stop their clicking, dusting and collecting, she looked at them and stood up perfectly straight as a man in a long black suit, shoes and a horrible blue tie walked in.

Amy had a good guess who he was, from everything she had seen about the senior positions in the Scottish Government, Amy could have sworn this was the Deputy First Minister (or deputy Prime Minister as he was now known). Even just that change in title made Amy smile and get excited, after decades of wanting freedom she was actually going to get it.

When the Deputy Prime Minister stopped and stared at Amy, she wasn't sure what to do exactly. The highest ranking person she had had the pleasure of seeing was the head of the police force, not a government person, so she had no idea what the protocol was here. Did she bow?

"Detective Sawkins?" he asked.

Amy waved her head at the crime scene techs to continue and she nodded. "Yes,"

"How goes the investigation?"

Amy was about to tell him she had only just arrived but the question that begged for her attention was why was the most powerful man in Scotland here?

"I thought you would be off celebrating Deputy Prime Minister," Amy said.

He smiled and gestured towards the broken safe. "Our freedom is useless unless we can keep it,"

Amy's eyes narrowed on him. That made no sense at all, Scotland was only a country of two, maybe three million people and despite the voting age being lowered to 16 years old, all the votes had been counted, validated and sent to London before early evening.

The vote was over, Scotland was free. What could go wrong?

"I'm sorry Sir but I don't understand," Amy said.

"Inside that safe were the original validation documents signed by the Counters, me and the First... Prime Minister of Scotland,"

Amy shrugged.

"We sent copies to London but they weren't happy. In a few hours the UK prime Minister is coming here personally to double check the results and if those documents aren't there then he will nullify the vote,"

Amy laughed, more out of shock than anything else. "What? He can't do that. The vote was fair, democratic and it wasn't rigged,"

The Deputy Prime Minister took a step closer to

Amy's ear. "I don't care that you aren't Scottish by blood. But you must know our history. From the Old Alliance with France to Scots trying to build an empire during the Colony times to much more recent political acts. Whenever Scotland tries to do much better than the English, the English damage us,"

Amy nodded. She had studied Scottish History at university and it was twisted, awful and beyond understanding, and he was right, whenever Scotland tried to do well for itself the English would create some law, send some order or do something else to stop them.

Amy was never going to allow the UK government to do that this time. She had to find those validation documents.

***

Half an hour later, Amy leant against the cold white window in her office as she watched the massive street parties in Edinburgh. People were jammed packed in the high street, dancing, singing and celebrating life. Then even Amy's favourite attraction, Edinburgh Castle, was firing firework after firework in a stunning array of colours.

Amy couldn't fail her people.

Amy forced herself away from the window and sat at her massive oak table and looked at her computer. She clicked on the rushed lab results from the break-in and she was hardly impressed.

She wanted the criminal to make some kind of mistake, something that would allow her to save

Scotland and go to the party she had wanted to go to quickly.

That clearly wasn't going to happen.

The results showed a few partial prints, some black fibres from the safe and some drops of blood on the shattered glass. To normal people that might have sounded like a lot of evidence to go on, but Amy had been doing this far too long now to know better than to get her hopes up.

According to the lab reports, the blood belonged to a white man and that was it. Unless Amy could find someone to compare the blood to it was as good as a paper coat in a storm, and as for the black fibres they were just your standard black tracksuit.

But something that Amy couldn't understand was why the criminal would want the validation papers? That knowledge was specialised at best, she was well educated and studied election law for a term at university, but she still didn't know that validation documents were important.

She certainly didn't know the UK Government would claim an election was invalid and nullify it.

Amy stood up and paced around her office for a while as she wondered who would know about the documents. It had to be someone within the government or someone working for the UK Government. Just the idea of that was disgusting, the vote was 80% in favour of independence so the idea someone from the minority would want to stop a democratic process was awful.

It was one of the reasons why she voted to leave, she didn't want to be ruled by a government Scotland didn't have the power to elect, but she knew some people preferred this fake democracy.

"Hello," a man said from Amy's door.

When Amy looked up at him, she instantly smiled as she stared at the beautiful smooth face and fit body of her stunning boyfriend Peter. She loved how his tight jeans and blue shirt left little to the imagination, she was definitely lucky in having him to herself.

And it was useful he was a detective too.

"Thought you were partying with our friends?" Amy asked.

Peter walked in and kissed her. "I couldn't leave you alone tonight. A crime scene tech filled me in and asked me to make you check your emails,"

Amy's eyebrows rose and she clicked on her emails to see a brand-new one with an attachment from an officer that she knew worked with the techs a fair bit.

"Look at this," Amy said as she opened the video clip in the email.

As Amy played it, she couldn't believe it as she saw two men dressed in black kick in the reinforced glass window and break into the safe. At first she couldn't believe it, because how would two men be able to shatter a reinforced window with just their kicks?

Then Peter pointed to the types of boots they

were wearing. "Steel toe-cap. I recognise the brand from what my brother worn back in the day,"

Amy frowned as Peter gently pushed her aside and started searching for more security footage on her computer.

But it was all still bothering Amy how the criminals knew about the validation documents, she was convinced that was the key and as Amy replayed the footage mentally she realised the criminals didn't double check if they had the right address. They knew exactly when to kick, attack and extract the documents from.

This was a professional job.

Somewhere in the back of Amy's mind she started to think about MI5 starting to interfere and wanting to destroy the legitimacy of the election, it was possible. But unlikely, surely?

"Here," Peter said, as he played a new piece of footage.

As he played the new footage for her, Amy focused on the images of the two men in their black tracksuits walking away from the street parties and towards a rather old stone house in Edinburgh.

It was definitely in the more expensive areas of the City and for some reason Amy just doubted these two criminals had enough money to buy a house in the neighbourhood, which only confirmed what Amy feared most.

That someone from the government was behind this.

"Who lives there?" Amy asked.

Peter did a quick search and frowned. "The Deputy Prime Minister,"

Amy felt her stomach flip, tense and churn as everything she feared was coming true.

But Amy had to stop the plan, recover the documents and made sure Scotland stayed free.

No matter the cost.

***

Thankfully it didn't take long for Amy and Peter to get to the house and the Deputy Prime Minister had led them into his office. Amy hated its cold brown wooden walls and desk but at least he had a plentiful supply of fine Scottish Whiskey in his cabinets.

Amy was a little surprised he was still in his black business suit, shoes and blue tie but he leant against his desk and smiled at them both.

Amy frowned. "We have video footage of two criminals who broke into the safe coming here. Where are the documents?"

His eyes widened. "I don't have them,"

Amy shot forward. "Don't lie to me! We have fought too hard for this to happen! Where are the documents!"

The Deputy Prime Minister smiled a little. "Please call me Ian and maybe you are more Scottish than me after all, but I promise you I didn't do this,"

Peter started to look around the office, and Amy's eyes kept narrowing on Ian, but she wasn't convinced. It wouldn't be the first time a Scottish Politician had tried to stop independence for their own strange delusions for so-called Great Britain.

"Detective Sawkins," Peter said as he held up documents and when Amy took them and started reading. She was shocked to find these were the validation documents.

"Deputy Prime Minister I am arresting you for theft of government property, treason and espionage against the People of Scotland-" Amy said.

But as she continued to read Ian his rights, he kept protesting his innocence and how he was being framed for the crime, and as Peter cuffed him, she just stopped.

It made no sense really. It made no sense to Amy why Ian would come to the crime scene, tell her about the importance of the case and then leave the documents in such an easy place to find.

Over the years Amy had heard plenty of times how the anti-independence folks had wanted to kill, steal and fight their way to remain part of the United Kingdom, so was it really that far to think they would frame a leading politician for theft?

And Amy remembered seeing Ian in all the different news reports, campaigns and everything leading up to the election, Ian and the First Minister were the two most famous people in the UK at this point. Amy couldn't believe he was hiding all this love for the UK by acting like someone who respectfully hated it.

Something else had to be going on.

"Stop," Amy said as Peter started to lead him out of the office. "Ian who else was here tonight?"

Peter frowned. "What you doing?"

"Protecting the people I serve," Amy said with a grin. "Ian the question?"

"No one else really. A friend popped round earlier. A fellow Politician," Ian said with a deepening frown. "And he wanted me to check my cellar for premium whiskey, I left the office for five minutes,"

Amy just shook her head at all of this. She was fuming, furious and rageful that some politician dared to defy the will of the Scottish people, and for what? His own ambitions, greed or delusions?

"I need a name," Amy said coldly.

As Peter undid the handcuffs and released Ian, he shrugged. "I only know him by his role in the Scottish Parliament,"

Amy's smile deepened. "That's all I need,"

"The Presiding Officer," Ian said.

Amy's blood went cold. That was one of the most important roles in the entire parliament, in the UK parliament and USA Congress people would call him the Speaker of the House, but this was awful that he would abuse his position to such an extreme degree.

Ian's phone went, he looked at it and his face went white.

"What it is?" Amy asked.

"You have to go now! The UK Prime Minister is

at the Scottish Parliament,"

Amy and Peter just looked at each other. They had to solve this now. They had to hurry or everything would end before it began.

"Delay him as long as you can!" Amy shouted to Ian as they all ran out the door.

***

Amy sat in a cold silver interrogation room as she stared at the Presiding Officer, it sickened her that such an important person in Scottish politics would dare to commit such a crime.

To Amy this still wasn't just some typical theft, it was a crime against her, her people and the kingdom of Scotland. This was the worse criminal act she had ever seen, and this criminal mastermind had to pay!

"Why do it?" Amy asked.

As Amy stared at the man called the presiding Officer, she wanted to spit at his smooth handsome face and strip him of his official posh clothing. It was a disgrace that he was still wearing the clothes of his office. The office he disgraced.

He wasn't speaking.

Amy checked his name on the file in front of her. "Presiding Officer Andrew McKinnon, why do it?"

He grinned at her. "I know the Prime Minister is here. All I have to do is stay quiet and in the end the UK government will nullify the vote. I have won,"

Amy didn't want to believe what she was hearing. "That will not happen. The people will never allow it,"

"Really? What if rumours circulated about the First Minister faking the results?"

Amy just shook her head. Scottish people weren't stupid, they would easily see through any deception, she hoped.

"Why don't I ask the two men you hired to tell me what happened?" Amy asked coldly.

"You don't have them. I had them send me a picture when they were on the train to London,"

Amy smiled and clicked her fingers. She never needed a confession, she just needed something to give her bosses, her people and the English to show criminals were behind it.

She was about to get up when her phone buzzed. Amy checked it and it was a text from Peter saying they needed more.

"Why would you send them to London?"

"I never sent them anywhere," Mr McKinnon said with an edge of fear in his voice.

"Why do it at all? You're a politician, you worked hard to get to your position, why…" Amy said.

But that was the key, he was a politician first and foremost, and as she lived in England for over twenty years, and served as a cop in London, she learnt a lot about the corruption of UK politics.

Amy almost didn't want to think about it, but it was perfectly reasonable to imagine the UK's bad habit slipping into Scottish politics, so someone had to pay, bride or even offer Mr McKinnon something.

"If I order my people to check your finances,

what will they find?" Amy asked.

Mr McKinnon shook a little. "I am innocent. The UK would never allow me to be put on trial,"

Amy could only smile at that. "You are not innocent. And the UK government has no jurisdiction here anymore. You are going to be trialled here and be the first person to be done by the Kingdom of Scotland,"

Mr McKinnon's breathing increased.

"If you confess now, I will help-"

The door opened, Peter and black masked men walked into the interrogation room. They grabbed Mr McKinnon and took him out the room.

"Stop!" Amy shouted.

Peter grabbed her and hugged her as tight as he could. "Don't Amy. Orders come from the Prime Minister herself, Mr McKinnon will be given over to the UK government in exchange for a better divorce deal,"

Amy wanted to lash out, shout and scream at the world for this idiot and everything he had almost cost her, but she couldn't. Because if the UK government was truly behind this and she had caught them, then Scotland's freedom was guaranteed.

The UK didn't need any more scandal already so Amy knew England would release Scotland easily enough with good terms and minimal hate.

And that was fine by her.

She had won hers, her people and her country's freedom in the nick of time.

And how many people could say that.

***

As she took off her clothes and pulled the wonderfully soft bedding over herself and her stunning boyfriend, Amy felt the Scottish flags that someone had painted on her at the street party and she really couldn't be bothered to take them off.

Amy listened to the final few fireworks, the last remnants of the party crowd staggering home and the laughing die down as everyone realised it was five o'clock in the morning, and they needed to head back.

But Amy was proud of herself and her stunning sexy boyfriend, and everything felt right about the world. They had had an amazing night of partying, drinking and food with each other, their families and friends, and for the first time in her life, Amy felt like everything was going to get better.

Because of her and her boyfriend, Scotland was now free to do whatever it wanted. She knew it wouldn't be easy sailing, there would be more political battles for the government to fight and they'll be ups and downs.

But that didn't matter to Amy.

Because finally Amy and every other Scot in the Kingdom had a chance to decide what they wanted to do, instead of someone they never elected deciding for them.

And that made Amy really excited about the future, but until then she would do what she always did. She would protect, serve and love her boyfriend, her family and her adoptive people.

Because when she lived in such a great place like Scotland, why wouldn't she?

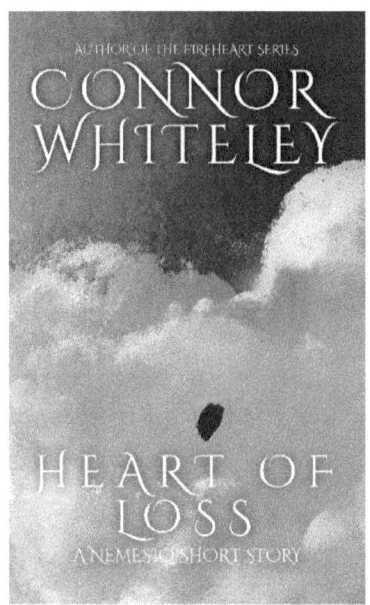

GET YOUR FREE AND EXCLUSIVE SHORT STORY NOW! LEARN ABOUT NEMESIO'S PAST!

https://www.subscribepage.com/fireheart

Keep up to date with exclusive deals on Connor Whiteley's Books, as well as the latest news about new releases and so much more!

Sign up for the Grab a Book and Chill Monthly newsletter, and you'll get one **FREE** ebook just for signing up: Agents of The Emperor Collection.

Sign Up Now!

https://dl.bookfunnel.com/f4p5xkprbk

https://www.subscribepage.com/psychologyboxset

About the author:

Connor Whiteley is the author of over 60 books in the sci-fi fantasy, nonfiction psychology and books for writer's genre and he is a Human Branding Speaker and Consultant.

He is a passionate warhammer 40,000 reader, psychology student and author.

Who narrates his own audiobooks and he hosts The Psychology World Podcast.

All whilst studying Psychology at the University of Kent, England.

Also, he was a former Explorer Scout where he gave a speech to the Maltese President in August 2018 and he attended Prince Charles' 70th Birthday Party at Buckingham Palace in May 2018.

Plus, he is a self-confessed coffee lover!

MYSTERY SHORT STORY COLLECTION VOUME 1

OTHER SHORT STORIES BY CONNOR WHITELEY

Blade of The Emperor
Arbiter's Truth
The Bloodied Rose
Asmodia's Wrath
Heart of A Killer
Emissary of Blood
Computation of Battle
Old One's Wrath
Puppets and Masters
Ship of Plague
Interrogation
Edge of Failure
One Way Choice
Acceptable Losses
Balance of Power
Good Idea At The Time
Escape Plan
Escape In The Hesitation
Inspiration In Need
Singing Warriors
Dragon Coins
Dragon Tea
Dragon Rider
Knowledge is Power
Killer of Polluters

Climate of Death
Sacrifice of the Soul
Heart of The Flesheater
Heart of The Regent
Heart of The Standing
Feline of The Lost
Heart of The Story
The Family Mailing Affair
Defining Criminality
The Martian Affair
A Cheating Affair
The Little Café Affair
Mountain of Death
Prisoner's Fight
Claws of Death
Bitter Air
Honey Hunt
Blade On A Train
City of Fire
Awaiting Death
Poison In The Candy Cane
Christmas Innocence
You Better Watch Out
Christmas Theft
Trouble In Christmas
Smell of The Lake
Problem In A Car

MYSTERY SHORT STORY COLLECTION VOUME 1

Theft, Past and Team
Embezzler In The Room
A Strange Way To Go
A Horrible Way To Go
Ann Awful Way To Go
An Old Way To Go
A Fishy Way To Go
A Pointy Way To Go
A High Way To Go
A Fiery Way To Go
A Glassy Way To Go
A Chocolatey Way To Go
Kendra Detective Mystery Collection Volume 1
Kendra Detective Mystery Collection Volume 2
Stealing A Chance At Freedom
Glassblowing and Death
Theft of Independence
Cookie Thief
Marble Thief
Book Thief
Art Thief
Mated At The Morgue
The Big Five Whoopee Moments
Stealing An Election
Mystery Short Story Collection Volume 1

Mystery Short Story Collection Volume 2

Other books by Connor Whiteley:
Bettie English Private Eye Series
A Very Private Woman
The Russian Case
A Very Urgent Matter
A Case Most Personal
Trains, Scots and Private Eyes
The Federation Protects

The Fireheart Fantasy Series
Heart of Fire
Heart of Lies
Heart of Prophecy
Heart of Bones
Heart of Fate

City of Assassins (Urban Fantasy)
City of Death
City of Marytrs
City of Pleasure
City of Power

MYSTERY SHORT STORY COLLECTION VOUME 1

<u>Agents of The Emperor</u>
Return of The Ancient Ones
Vigilance
Angels of Fire
Kingmaker
The Eight

<u>The Garro Series- Fantasy/Sci-fi</u>
GARRO: GALAXY'S END
GARRO: RISE OF THE ORDER
GARRO: END TIMES
GARRO: SHORT STORIES
GARRO: COLLECTION
GARRO: HERESY
GARRO: FAITHLESS
GARRO: DESTROYER OF WORLDS
GARRO: COLLECTIONS BOOK 4-6
GARRO: MISTRESS OF BLOOD
GARRO: BEACON OF HOPE
GARRO: END OF DAYS

<u>Winter Series- Fantasy Trilogy Books</u>
WINTER'S COMING
WINTER'S HUNT
WINTER'S REVENGE
WINTER'S DISSENSION

Miscellaneous:
RETURN
FREEDOM
SALVATION
Reflection of Mount Flame
The Masked One
The Great Deer

<u>All books in 'An Introductory Series':</u>
BIOLOGICAL PSYCHOLOGY 3RD EDITION
COGNITIVE PSYCHOLOGY THIRD EDITION
SOCIAL PSYCHOLOGY- 3RD EDITION
ABNORMAL PSYCHOLOGY 3RD EDITION
PSYCHOLOGY OF RELATIONSHIPS- 3RD EDITION
DEVELOPMENTAL PSYCHOLOGY 3RD EDITION
HEALTH PSYCHOLOGY
RESEARCH IN PSYCHOLOGY
A GUIDE TO MENTAL HEALTH AND TREATMENT AROUND THE WORLD- A GLOBAL LOOK AT DEPRESSION
FORENSIC PSYCHOLOGY
THE FORENSIC PSYCHOLOGY OF THEFT, BURGLARY AND OTHER CRIMES AGAINST PROPERTY
CRIMINAL PROFILING: A FORENSIC PSYCHOLOGY GUIDE TO FBI PROFILING AND GEOGRAPHICAL AND STATISTICAL PROFILING.
CLINICAL PSYCHOLOGY
FORMULATION IN PSYCHOTHERAPY

PERSONALITY PSYCHOLOGY AND INDIVIDUAL DIFFERENCES
CLINICAL PSYCHOLOGY REFLECTIONS VOLUME 1
CLINICAL PSYCHOLOGY REFLECTIONS VOLUME 2
CULT PSYCHOLOGY
Police Psychology

Companion guides:
BIOLOGICAL PSYCHOLOGY 2ND EDITION WORKBOOK
COGNITIVE PSYCHOLOGY 2ND EDITION WORKBOOK
SOCIOCULTURAL PSYCHOLOGY 2ND EDITION WORKBOOK
ABNORMAL PSYCHOLOGY 2ND EDITION WORKBOOK
PSYCHOLOGY OF HUMAN RELATIONSHIPS 2ND EDITION WORKBOOK
HEALTH PSYCHOLOGY WORKBOOK
FORENSIC PSYCHOLOGY WORKBOOK

www.ingramcontent.com/pod-product-compliance
Lightning Source LLC
LaVergne TN
LVHW012126070526
838202LV00056B/5878